D0561674

1 2 3 4 5 6 7 8 9 10

❖

First Edition

RAINBOW FISH
FINDERS KEEPERS

HarperFestival®

A Division of HarperCollins*Publishers*

Rainbow Fish was swimming

through the Coral Reef.

He was looking for colorful

shells for his collection.

What could that be? Rainbow Fish wondered.

He swam down for a closer look.

"It's so bright and shiny."

"Sea glass!" cried Rainbow Fish.

"It's so beautiful."

Rainbow Fish loved the sea glass.

He always carried it around—

pretty sea glass, with a hole in it.

One day after school,

Rainbow Fish couldn't find his sea glass.

"Oh, no! How could I have lost it?" he cried

He searched every inch of the Coral Reef.

He looked everywhere but could not find it.

It wasn't at the Sunken Ship

or swirling in the Whirlpool.

It wasn't along Mrs. Crabbitz's shortcut.

Rainbow Fish was heartbroken.

His beautiful sea glass was gone.

A few days later, Little Blue jetted
through the Sunken Ship.

"Check out my lucky charm," he boasted.

"Hey, that's my sea glass!"

cried Rainbow Fish.

"I've been looking all over for it.

Where did you find it?"

14

"It's not your sea glass," said Little Blue.

"Yes it is. I found it and then I lost it,"
said Rainbow Fish.

"I've had this forever," said Little Blue.

"Oh, come on Little Blue," said Rosie.

"I saw you pick that up at the Oyster Beds

on the way to school."

"I must have dropped it at the
Oyster Beds when I went looking
for pearls with Puffer," said
Rainbow Fish.

"That doesn't prove anything!
Just because you lost a piece of sea glass
doesn't mean that this one is yours,"
cried Little Blue.

"Besides," said Little Blue,

"I've never seen you

with a piece of sea glass."

"I have an idea," said Dyna
as she took the piece of sea glass
and hid it behind her.

"Describe the sea glass to me,"

said Dyna.

"Little Blue, you start."

Little Blue hesitated.

"Well . . . it's um orange . . ." he said.

"You mean red," Rainbow Fish corrected.

"Right. That's what I meant. Red!"
Little Blue said.

"And it's . . . smooth and round,"
Little Blue added.

"You mean except for the hole,"
Rainbow Fish corrected.

"Of course. Except for the hole,"

said Little Blue.

"I got mixed up when you interrupted me."

"That's not what it sounds like to me," said Dyna.

Everyone agreed that the sea glass belonged to Rainbow Fish.

"I found it, fair and square!"

shouted Little Blue.

"Finders keepers, losers weepers!"

"What if you lost something
you really loved?" asked Dyna.
"But it's not fair," cried Little Blue.

"Maybe Rainbow Fish could help
you find another piece of sea
glass," suggested Tug.

"We'll never find a piece of sea glass like this one," said Little Blue.

"We can find one that's just as pretty,"

said Rainbow Fish.

"You can hold this one while we look."

Little Blue found a piece of sea glass.

It was bright yellow and very pretty.

Rainbow Fish had his own sea glass back.

They were both very happy.